A Christmas Carol

Charles Dickens
Adapted by Lesley Sims

Illustrated by
Alan Marks

Reading Consultant: Alison Kelly
University of Surrey Roehampton

Contents

Chapter 1

Scrooge and Marley

Marley was dead, dead as a doornail. All that remained of the firm of **Scrooge and Marley** was Ebenezer Scrooge.

Scrooge... a grasping, greedy, gruesome old man! He was as hard as stone, and so cold inside his face looked frozen.

Scrooge didn't care for anyone and hardly anyone cared for him. Even Christmas cheer couldn't thaw his icy heart.

One Christmas Eve, he was busy in his counting house. He had left his office door open, to keep an eye on his clerk, Bob Cratchit.

"A Merry Christmas, Uncle!" cried a cheerful voice suddenly. It was Scrooge's nephew, Fred.

"Bah, humbug!" said Scrooge.

What right have you to be merry? You're poor!

What right have you to be miserable? You're rich!

"If I had my way," Scrooge added, "every idiot who said 'Merry Christmas' would be cooked with his own cake!"

"Really, Uncle!" cried Fred. "Come, why not eat with us tomorrow?"

"Good afternoon!" Scrooge replied, returning to his books.

As Fred left, two other men came in, collecting for the poor.

"Are there no prisons?" asked Scrooge. "No workhouses? I pay for those. That's enough."

The men went out into the bitterly cold afternoon, shaking their heads. A little later, a scruffy boy paused by Scrooge's office and began to sing.

God bless you, merry gentlemen...

But one look at Scrooge and he fled without finishing the verse.

Finally, it was time to go home.

"You'll want the whole day off tomorrow, I suppose?" Scrooge snapped at Bob.

"If it's convenient," said Bob.

"It isn't. Be here all the earlier the day after."

Scrooge left the office with a
growl. Bob quickly locked up and
set off for home. Scrooge went
for his usual lonely dinner in a
lonely inn.

Then he too set off for home, a
few gloomy rooms in an old house
which once belonged to Marley.

Chapter 2

Marley's ghost

The door knocker on this house was not unusual, just large. But, as Scrooge put his key in the door, the knocker changed into Marley's face.

Startled, Scrooge turned his key
and went in. Was the back of
Marley's head sticking out into the
hall? No, he saw only screws.

"Pah, humbug!" he said, closing
the door with a bang. But he
checked all his rooms, just in case,
before he got ready for bed.

Without warning, an old bell began to ring. It started quietly but soon rang loudly, along with every other bell in the house. Suddenly, the bells stopped. A clanking noise followed, as if someone in the cellar was dragging a chain.

Then, slowly, something came through the door...

Marley's ghost?
It can't be!

Scrooge could not believe it.
"Why don't you believe your
eyes?" asked the ghost.
"Because even an upset stomach
can disturb the senses," Scrooge told
him. "Maybe the milk was sour and
it's giving me a nightmare."
The ghost let out a frightful cry
and rattled its chains.

14

"Mercy!" cried Scrooge. "Why do you trouble me?" Again, the ghost shook its chains. "And why are you chained up?" Scrooge added.

"These chains are a punishment for my selfish life," said the ghost. "There are some waiting for you, too, and getting heavier every day."

But you were so good at business!

My only business should have been taking care of others.

"I've come here tonight to warn you," said the ghost. "You might escape my fate."

Scrooge looked relieved.

"You will be haunted by three spirits," the ghost went on.

"I think I'd rather not," said Scrooge.

The ghost ignored him and headed for the window.

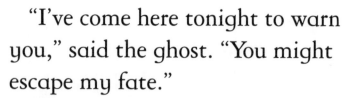

Expect the first spirit when the clock chimes one.

Scrooge closed the window and checked his door. It was still locked. "Humb–" he began, but the word stuck in his throat.

Worn out – partly from shock, partly because it was two in the morning – Scrooge fell into bed. He was asleep in an instant.

Chapter 3

The first spirit

Scrooge awoke in total darkness.
To his surprise, a clock chimed
twelve. He lay awake, fearfully
counting down the next hour. On
the stroke of one, a hand drew
back the curtain around his bed...

Scrooge gasped. He was face to face with the strangest creature he had ever seen. A light shone out of its head and it carried a cap like a candle snuffer.

"Are you the spirit I was told about?" he asked.

"I am!" said the ghost, softly. "I'm the Ghost of Christmas Past... your past."

Rise and walk with me!

Scrooge clung to the spirit as he floated through the window and out... not into the foggy city but a bright, cold day in the country.

"I was a boy here," Scrooge cried. The ghost took him to his old schoolroom where a lonely boy sat alone.

Before he knew it, they were back in a busy city and entering a warehouse, where a party was in full swing.

"And here I was an apprentice!" cried Scrooge. "There's my master, old Fezziwig. He made us so happy..."

The party faded, leaving Scrooge and the spirit outside. There was the young Scrooge again, sitting beside a beautiful girl.

"I cannot marry you," she said, sadly. "You love money more than you love me."

Spirit! Show me no more...

One shadow more. Watch!

The scene changed and Scrooge found himself in a comfy room, filled with children. There was his old love, now married to another man.

Spirit, remove me! I cannot bear it.

This is what happened. Do not blame me!

Scrooge began to struggle with the ghost. As he did, he noticed the light on its head burning even more brightly. Scrooge grabbed the spirit's cap and put it over the light, pressing hard.

The spirit sank down and Scrooge sank into a deep sleep.

Chapter 4

The second spirit

Scrooge woke up, back in bed, as a clock struck one. He sat up nervously but nothing happened. He flung back his curtains. No one was there.

Finally, Scrooge got up and went
into the next room. He could
hardly recognize it. And right in
the middle sat the second spirit.

Scrooge followed the ghost, through streets full of people preparing for Christmas. Finally, they came to Bob Cratchit's house, where Mrs. Cratchit was getting the Christmas dinner ready.

Where are your father and Tiny Tim?

"Here's father!" cried the two youngest, as Bob came in, carrying his invalid son.

Soon, everyone was enjoying the feast. It was a small meal for such a large family but no one would have dreamed of saying so.

A Merry Christmas to us all!

God bless us, every one!

"Spirit," said Scrooge suddenly, "tell me if Tiny Tim will live."

"I see an empty seat," said the ghost. "If things stay as they are, he will die."

Scrooge felt terrible, but then he heard his name.

"To Mr. Scrooge, who provided our feast!" cried Bob.

"Provided our feast, indeed!" snorted his wife. "I wish he was here. I'd give him a piece of my mind to feast upon."

By now, it was getting dark.
The ghost led Scrooge back
outside, into the bustling streets.
They flew to quieter, emptier
places... but everywhere Scrooge
saw people full of Christmas spirit.

31

In the midst of the gloom,
Scrooge heard a hearty laugh. It
was his nephew Fred. They had
arrived in the middle of Fred's
Christmas dinner party.

"I feel sorry for Scrooge," said Fred. "Now, how about a game of blind man's buff?"

One game followed another. Scrooge grew so excited, he joined in, though no one could see or hear him.

Scrooge wanted to stay until the last guest left, but the ghost said no. "Just one more game then," Scrooge pleaded. "It's a new one called 'Yes and No'."

"Scrooge it is!" cried Fred. "And I wish him a Merry Christmas, whatever he is."

Before Scrooge could wish Fred the same, the ghost had whisked him away. They went all over the world, finding rejoicing and hope. But the ghost was growing old.

"My life is brief," the spirit explained. "It ends at midnight."

Already the clock was chiming three quarters past eleven.

"Forgive me for asking," said Scrooge, "but is something hidden in your robes?"

"Look," the ghost replied, revealing two miserable children. "The boy is Ignorance, the girl is Want. Beware of them both, but especially the boy!"

"Have they nowhere to go?" asked Scrooge.

"Are there no prisons? No workhouses?" the spirit replied, using Scrooge's own words.

The clock struck twelve and the spirit vanished. As the last chime died away, Scrooge saw a hooded phantom coming closer.

Chapter 5

The last spirit

The phantom floated silently up to Scrooge.

"Are you the Ghost of Christmas Yet To Come?" he asked.

The phantom said nothing, but pointed its ghostly hand.

"Ghost of the future," cried Scrooge, "I fear you more than any other, but I shall go with you."

Staying silent, the ghost glided off. As Scrooge followed, a city seemed to spring up around them.

They left the crowds and went to a part of town Scrooge had never visited. As they entered a junk store, three people came in with things to sell.

Scrooge was horrified. These things had been stolen from a dead man's house.

"Spirit, I see!" he cried. "This poor man might be me."

As he spoke, the scene changed. Now, they were in a bedroom. A dead man lay on the bed, alone but for a cat and some rats. The phantom pointed to the man's face, but Scrooge couldn't look.

"Is no one moved by this man's death?" he begged.

The phantom spread out his dark robe for a second. When he drew it back, Scrooge saw a room where a man and wife were talking.

"We owe him so much money," the woman said. "It would take a miracle to soften his heart."

"It's past softening," replied her husband, cheerfully. "He's dead!"

"But they are happy!" said
Scrooge. "Let me see some sorrow
for a death, spirit, please."

The phantom took him to the
Cratchits' house. Mrs. Cratchit and
her children were by the fire. An
air of sadness hung over them.

As Scrooge watched them, he had the feeling that the phantom was about to leave.

"Before you go, tell me, who was the man on the bed?" he begged.

The phantom said nothing but took Scrooge to a churchyard.

"He lies here?" said Scrooge. Silently, the ghost pointed to a gravestone.

"Answer me one question, then," asked Scrooge. "Have I seen what will happen or what might happen?"

Still the ghost remained silent.

Trembling all over, Scrooge crept
up to the gravestone and read the
name upon it.

EBENEZER
SCROOGE

With a terrible cry, Scrooge grabbed the ghost's robe. "No, spirit. Oh no!"

But the phantom simply pointed to Scrooge and back to the grave.

"I'm not the man I was," Scrooge cried. "Let me change."

Scrooge closed his eyes to pray. When he opened them again, the phantom had become his bedpost.

Chapter 6

Merry Christmas!

He was back in his own bed.

"Ha!" he laughed. "I'm as light as a feather, as merry as a school boy. Thank you, Marley! From now on, I'll keep Christmas in my heart all year round."

"I don't know what day it is. I don't know what month it is! I don't care," he babbled. Just then, the church bells rang out. Scrooge raced to his window.

What's today, boy?

Today? Why, Christmas Day!

The spirits had done all their work in one night.

Scrooge chuckled and sent the boy off to buy the butcher's prize turkey. "I'll send it to Bob Cratchit," he said to himself and rubbed his hands with glee. "It's twice the size of Tiny Tim!"

When the boy returned with the turkey, Scrooge gasped. The bird was huge. "Will you deliver it for me?" he asked, chuckling some more. "You'll need a cab."

And he paid the boy, found a cab and went back inside, still chuckling. He chuckled until the tears rolled down his cheeks.

At last, he was dressed in his best and outside. He looked so cheerful that several people said, "Morning sir! Merry Christmas!" Scrooge thought those the most beautiful words he had ever heard.

He hadn't gone far when he met the men who had been collecting for the poor the day before.

"Merry Christmas!" he cried. The two men looked shocked. Was this Scrooge?

Forgive me for being so rude. Come to my office and I'll make it up to you.

Feeling better, Scrooge went to church and then for a walk. He had never felt so happy.

In the afternoon, he went to his nephew Fred's house. He went up to the door a dozen times before he dared knock.

Fred welcomed him to the party with such delight, Scrooge felt at home in five minutes.

It was a wonderful party. But
Scrooge was at work early next
day. He wanted to catch Bob
Cratchit coming in late. And he
did. Bob was nearly twenty
minutes late.

And just what
do you mean
by this?

Scrooge pretended to be furious.
"I'm not going to stand for it any
longer! Step into my office."

"It's only once a year," said Bob.

"I'll tell you what I'm going to do," Scrooge went on, poking him in the ribs, "I'm going to raise your salary. Merry Christmas, Bob! Now, put some more coal on the fire before you pick up your quill!"

Scrooge promised to take care of Bob and his family, and he was as good as his word. To Tiny Tim – who did not die – he was a second father. Not only that, he became a good friend to all who lived in his town.

Hello Scrooge! Hello Tim! Lovely day!

Some people laughed to see the change in him. Scrooge just let them laugh. He didn't care. He knew laughing was good for them and his own heart laughed with them.

He never saw the spirits again
but it was always said of him that
he knew how to have a jolly
Christmas. May that be true of all
of us. And so, in the words of Tiny
Tim, "God bless us, every one!"

There are lots more great stories for you to read:

Usborne Young Reading: Series One
Aladdin and his Magical Lamp
Animal Legends
Stories of Dragons
Stories of Giants
Stories of Gnomes & Goblins
Stories of Magical Animals
Stories of Pirates
Stories of Princes & Princesses
Stories of Witches
The Burglar's Breakfast
The Dinosaurs Next Door
The Monster Gang
Wizards

Usborne Young Reading: Series Two
Aesop's Fables
Gulliver's Travels
Jason & The Golden Fleece
Robinson Crusoe
The Adventures of King Arthur
The Amazing Adventures of Hercules
The Amazing Adventures of Ulysses
The Clumsy Crocodile
The Fairground Ghost
The Incredible Present
Treasure Island

Designed by
Russell Punter

First published in 2003 by Usborne Publishing Ltd.,
Usborne House, 83-85 Saffron Hill, London EC1N 8RT,
England. www.usborne.com
This edition first published in 2004.
Copyright © 2003 Usborne Publishing Ltd.